Most Loved in All the World

by **Tonya Cherie Hegamin**

illustrated by **Cozbi A. Cabrera**

Houghton Mifflin Company

BOSTON 2009

www.houghtonmifflinbooks.com
The text of this book is set in 16-point Regula Antiqua.
The illustrations are done in acrylic paint and textile collaging.
Book design by Carol Goldenberg

Library of Congress Cataloging-in-Publication Data
Hegamin, Tonya Cherie.
Most loved in all the world / by Tonya Cherie Hegamin ; illustrated by Cozbi A. Cabrera.
p. cm.
Summary: Even though Mama is an agent on the Underground Railroad, in order to help others she must remain a
slave, but she teaches her daughter the value of freedom through a gift of love and sacrifice.
ISBN 0-618-41903-9
[1. Mother and child—Fiction. 2. Slavery—Fiction. 3. African Americans—Fiction.]
I. Cabrera, Cozbi A., ill. II. Title.
PZ7.H35885Mo 2008
[E]—dc22
2004013189
ISBN-13: 978-0-618-41903-6

Printed in China
SCP 10 9 8 7 6 5 4 3 2 1

To the ancestors of before
And the children of now

−T.C.H.

For my mother, Prisca, no stranger to sacrifice...

−C.A.C.

MAMA works hard in the field.

My hands are too little. My job is to bring water.

Mama's hands are bleeding 'cause she pick so much cotton.

I'm too little, but I wish I could help.

Toil time is over when the last light winks behind the trees.

Tonight I'll rub salve in Mama's cuts.

She come home and pick up her needle and thread.

Mama's gonna make a new quilt.

"This quilt for the Big House?"

Mama smile and say no.

"This quilt for Massa to sell?"

Mama smile and shake her head.

Mama so pretty by the fire; so dark, so strong.

She sew pieces handed down from the Big House.

She sew pieces she trade with folks from town.

She sew pieces of old clothes.

I watch Mama cut and stitch different shapes

till I fall asleep at her knee.

The sun rises to find Mama already in the field.

I wake soon after, find what she was making:

    a log cabin

    a star

    a brown tree with green on one side

    a little girl.

I wonder about that little girl,

her tiny embroidered face so happy.

Maybe her mama don't have to work no more.

Maybe her mama can stay all day and hold her close.

I think about that little cut-out girl

as I put on my dress,

as I run up to the Big House.

I'm too little to work the field; my job is to fetch and carry.

I think about Mama working so hard

as I bring water to the fields for the folks to drink.

Their backs are bent, their hands are cut.

I wonder how much salve it would take to heal them all.

Tonight when Mama come home
she have whip marks 'cross her back.
Tonight when Mama come home
she have tear marks down her face.

Still she pick up her needle and thread.
I ask: "Can I work with you tomorrow?
I'm gettin' big and strong. I'll work hard like you."
Mama look real sad and say no.

Her shirt is torn where the whip cut her back.
Mama takes off her shirt and cuts out a big heart,
puts it with the other shapes she made.
"What these shapes for?" I ask.

Mama smile and whisper in my ear: "A log cabin means a place is safe.
This star is brightest in the sky; it's for you to follow.
The moss should only be growin' on the side of the tree
in the direction you are headed."

"And the little girl?" I ask. "Why she so happy?"
Mama put her arm around me,
to squeeze me real tight. "This little girl," Mama say,
"is the most loved in all the world."

Some long nights later, Mama wakes me from sleeping.
She holds the quilt folded over her arm.
"You finish, Mama?" I ask out loud,
but she puts her finger to my mouth.

"We goin' to a meetin'," she whispers.

"Put on your clothes, quiet as you can."

We step out into the night like it has ears to hear us.

Mama holds my hand tight, leads me deep into the forest.

We creep to a clearing in the woods.
Mama makes a sound like I've never heard before—
she whistles clear and sweet, just like a bird.
Folks step out of the darkness.

There's folks I know, folks I never seen.
Folks from the Big House, folks from the field.
"You must go with these people, child," Mama says, bending close.
"I can't go with you, but they'll help you find Freedom."

There's a woman holding a small lantern;
she nods to Mama then reaches out to me.
I hide my face in Mama's skirts.
Don't want to leave her, my home.

Mama kneels and shows me the quilt:
a log cabin for safety
a star to follow
moss on the trees to lead.

And in the middle, a little girl so happy,
surrounded by a worn and tattered heart.
Mama wraps me in the quilt,
kisses me quick.

"Remember what I told you about Freedom?" she ask.

I remember: when nobody own nobody else.

When there is no thing as master and slave.

When Mama don't come home bleeding, whipped.

She pushes me to the woman. Tears fall like stars from Mama's eyes.

I remember Freedom, but what is it without Mama?

Who'll rub the salve in her hands?

Who'll bring water to the folks in the field?

"Why can't you come, too?" I cry. Mama turn and say:

"I got to stay, help others find Freedom."

The woman pulls me away; Mama points to the quilt and says:

"Don't forget what I told you."

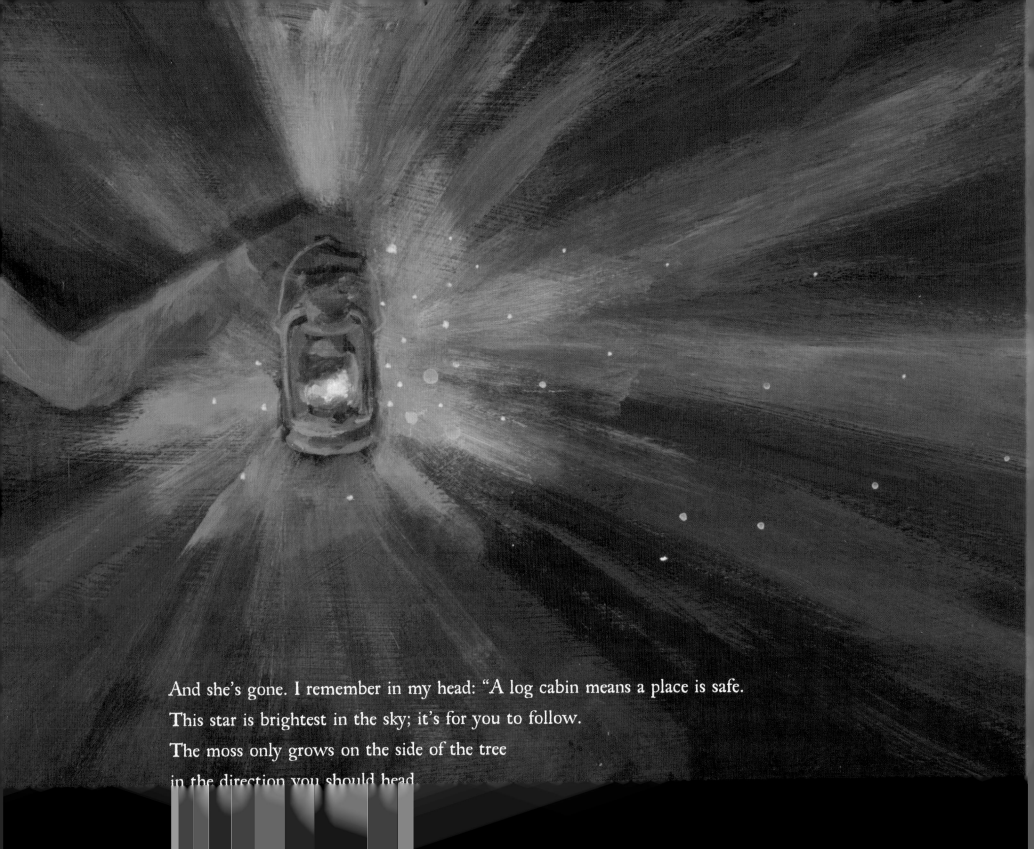

And she's gone. I remember in my head: "A log cabin means a place is safe.
This star is brightest in the sky; it's for you to follow.
The moss only grows on the side of the tree
in the direction you should head.

And this little girl
is the most loved in all the world."

Author's Note to Parents and Educators

ALTHOUGH IT MIGHT BE HARD for some people to understand how a mother could send a child off into the unknown without her, it was a common fact of slavery. Even in our modern times, for so many reasons, women are forced to do the same—give up their children for adoption or put them into foster care—not because they do not love the child, but often because they simply do not live in conditions in which they can give the child the life he or she deserves. In a way, these mothers place their love and value for their children's future over their own feelings. When I wrote this story, I envisioned a woman, a spy and secret agent on the Underground Railroad, a woman who valued freedom so much that she would desire her child's more than her own. Because the lives of the enslaved were so uncertain, for this woman there could be no false hope of reuniting, although she would desperately want to. Her only concern is that her daughter grows up free and far from the bonds of slavery. Although the documented history about the Underground Railroad has been cloaked, I believe there might have been many "secret agents" like the mother in this book who sacrificed being with their children for the greater good. I think that the hope in this story is that the little girl gets a chance at freedom knowing that her mother loved her and was unselfish enough to give her that chance even if it meant that they'd never see each other again.

Africans were fleeing not simply hard physical labor but more the spiritual torture and emotional toil of enslavement. The childhood death rate for slaves was two to three times higher than that for whites. Enslaved children who survived disease and malnutrition were not often raised by their birth families because of forced separation by slave owners and traders. Most children were put to hard labor (like carrying hundred-pound sacks of cotton) by age eight. Although there are a few accounts of whole families escaping on the Underground Railroad together, often, because of circumstance, parents would have to send their children north without them, regardless of overwhelming feelings of loss and regret, and without even a shred of hope of seeing their loved ones again. Their only hope was freedom itself.

The Underground Railroad transported an estimated one hundred thousand freedom seekers from the relentless fields of rice and cotton from about 1830 until around 1861. There were so many people who took part in this secret and illegal practice of stealing freedom—not only public figures like Harriet Tubman and Frederick Douglass but those whose job it was to stay on the plantation to encourage and help others to escape.

I've always wondered about those brave folks who would return to slavery or stay behind just to help others emancipate themselves. History tells us there were many people who did this. What sacrifice! And how would they raise their own children, knowing their fate as slaves? These folks saw slavery as an all-out war; they lived by the strict codes of true soldiers.

Some historians debate the use of quilts in the Underground Railroad, but I personally believe that enslaved Africans would have used their natural ingenuity to devise any and every method imaginable in their struggle for freedom. As quilt historian Xenia Cord has said, "Quilt research and quilt history often rely heavily on the oral anecdotes and oral memories of quilters, stories that link women with common interests to a body of shared information." I wanted to use the symbolism of quilting as a device to share information about slavery, not to document quilt use in the Underground Railroad as fact. In this story I used the symbols of the North Star and log cabin; however, I also reinterpreted symbols from African American folklore, like moss growing on the north side of trees, and translated it into a coded quilt square. Because the Underground Railroad system was indeed so complicated and covert, we may never know to what lengths people went to keep their efforts blanketed with mystery.

I thought of that harsh reality while reading about contemporary African American quilt styles and textiles. African patterns and symbols are still used by American quilters today, passed down through the generations. Enslaved Africans brought much of this intricate skill to the Americas with their hands and memories to pass down the knowledge of their people. In this way, I hope that *Most Loved in All the World* conveys a facet of the courage and sacrifice so many enslaved Africans willingly endured—for unconditional love and for freedom.

I could not have written this book without the enduring love and support of my family and my friends who are my family. I'd also like to especially thank Arnold Adoff and Andrea Davis Pinkney for helping me get my feet off the ground.

TONYA CHERIE HEGAMIN

Further Reading

Franklin, John Hope, and Alfred A. Moss, Jr. FROM SLAVERY TO FREEDOM: A HISTORY OF AFRICAN AMERICANS. New York: Knopf, 1947.

Tobin, Jacqueline L., and Raymond G. Dobard. HIDDEN IN PLAIN VIEW: A SECRET STORY OF QUILTS AND THE UNDERGROUND RAILROAD. New York: Doubleday, 1999.

Wahlman, Maude Southwell. SIGNS AND SYMBOLS: AFRICAN IMAGES IN AFRICAN AMERICAN QUILTS, second edition. Atlanta: Tinwood Books, 2001.

National Parks Service/National Underground Railroad Network to Freedom
www.crnps.gov/ugrr

National Underground Railroad Freedom Center
www.freedomcenter.org

The Atlantic Slave Trade and Slave Life in the Americas: A Visual Record
http://hitchcock.itc.virginia.edu/Slavery/

National Geographic News article; February 5, 2004
http://news.nationalgeographic.com/news/2004/02/0205_040205slavequilts.html

Xenia Cord, "Patches from the Past"
http://historyofquilts.com/underground-railroad.html